To Emma.
May all your Christmas
wishes come true!

Love....................................

Emma is **excited**
Christmastime is here!

She says, "I wish for lots and lots of fluffy snow this year!"

Emma writes to Santa.
The letter takes her ages.

"Perhaps I've wished for way too much?"
(There are over 50 pages!)

Dear Santa,

Emma decorates the tree
with twinkly lights that glow.

Christmas
decorations

Look at Emma up on stage.
She's in the Christmas play.

She wished to make
her family proud,
and have the greatest day!

The kitchen's very busy.
Emma smells cookies baking.

"I wish that I could eat that bowl of cookie dough Dad's making."

Emma wakes at 5 a.m.
"It's Christmas Day!
Yippee!"

She runs downstairs
to find a pile of
presents beneath
the tree.

This sweater's really **itchy**.
She tries to grin and bear it,
but Emma really wishes that
she didn't have to wear it!

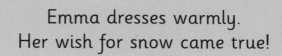

Emma dresses warmly.
Her wish for snow came true!

She's off to build a snowman now.
Perhaps she will build two!

Emma's sledding
down the hill,
"I wish I could
speed up!"

Her wish comes true,
her sled is *fast*
when powered by a pup!

It's after Christmas dinner,
and everyone is snoring.
Emma says to her best friend,
"I wish it was less **BORING!**"

Mom is asking Emma,
"Did your **BIGGEST** wish come true?"
"Oh yes," she smiles,
"that wish was being..."

"...here with **all** of you!"

Do you wish for fun with friends,
or a family trip that never ends?
Whatever it is that you hold dear,
keep your Christmas wishes here!

I wish...

Published by Put Me In The Story,
a publication of Sourcebooks, Inc.
P.O. Box 4410, Naperville, Illinois 60567-4410
(630) 961-3900
Fax: (630) 961-2168
www.putmeinthestory.com

Date of Production: August 2018
Run Number: HTW_PO201829
Printed and bound in China (GD)
10 9 8 7 6 5 4 3 2 1

put **me**
in the **story**®

Bestselling books starring your child!
www.putmeinthestory.com